UTOPIA

MINUS

AHSAHTA PRESS
THE NEW SERIES #39

UTOPIA MINUS

SUSAN BRIANTE

AHSAHTA PRESS
BOISE, IDAHO / 2011

Ahsahta Press, Boise State University
Boise, Idaho 83725-1525
http://ahsahtapress.boisestate.edu
http://ahsahtapress.boisestate.edu/books/briante2/briante2.htm

Copyright © 2011 by Susan Briante
Printed in the United States of America
Cover design by Quemadura
Book design by Janet Holmes
First printing March 2011

Library of Congress Cataloging-in-Publication Data

Briante, Susan.
Utopia minus / Susan Briante.
p. cm. -- (The new series ; #39)
ISBN-13: 978-1-934103-19-7 (pbk. : alk. paper)
ISBN-10: 1-934103-19-5 (pbk. : alk. paper)
I. Title.
PS3602.R485U86 2011
811'.6--DC22

                        2010043827

Acknowledgments appear on page 85.

for Farid Matuk

witness and guide through the demolitions and renovations
that made this book possible

"The zero panorama seemed to contain *ruins in reverse*, that is—all the new construction that would eventually be built. This is the opposite of the 'romantic ruin' because the buildings don't *fall* into ruin *after* they are built but rather *rise* into ruin before they are built. This anti-romantic *mise-en-scène* suggests the discredited idea of time and many other "out of date" things. But the suburbs exist without a rational past without the "big events" of history.... A Utopia minus a bottom, a place where the machines are idle, and the sun has turned to glass..."

ROBERT SMITHSON, *A Guide to the Monuments of Passaic New Jersey*

Contents

I.

The End of Another Creature   3
Texas Redbud   4
Jerusalem   5
11 Railway Lines Stretch from Chicago by 1861   6
Woodsmoke, Starbucks, Gettysburg   7
I-35   8
Texas State Fair   10
Notes from the Last Great Civil War Story   11
Sunset on the First Day of Standard Time   13
Nail Guns in the Morning   14
Chalk Marks on the Front Walk   16
Scrap Metal   17
Yellow Finches Drop from a Plane Tree   18
In the Field   19
Specimen Box   20
A Photograph from Nature   22

Memoranda

Dear Mr. Surgeon General   25
Dear Madam Secretary of Homeland Security   27
Dear Mr. Chairman of Ethics, Leadership and Personnel Policy in the
    U.S. Army's Office of the Deputy Chief of Staff for Personnel   29

II.

Isabella 33
Morning, Dump Truck, Arabesque 34
Here in the Mountains 36
From the Ruined Concrete Foundry West of Airport Blvd between
    Manor and M.L.K. 37
Robert Mueller Municipal Airport 38
Abandoned Commercial Use Property, 43rd and Ave. B 40
At the Lake 41
Red Constellations 42
3000 Block Kings Ln—Demolished Apartment Complex 43
Big Ideas 44
A Blackbird Lands on a Wind-Whipped Branch 45
From the Ruined Concrete Foundry West of Airport Blvd between
    Manor and M.L.K. 46
Public Transportation 47
Goodbye Twentieth Century 48
Mid-State 49

Memoranda

Dear Mr. Secretary of Housing and Urban Development 55
Dear Mr. Director of the Census Bureau 56
Dear Mr. President 58

III.

And Suddenly It's the First of the Month   61
Better than Paris   62
Hover   64
September's Company   66
Short Lines   67
Big Theory   68
December   69
From the Homefront   70
Other Denver Economies   71
Up the Road   73
Peach Tree   74
Windows, Roof, Wood   77
A Letter to Eileen Myles   79
Alexander Litvinenko   81

Notes   83
About the Author   85

I.

The End of Another Creature

Starlings in the magnolia tree crackle, static, lightning; a helicopter floats overhead. Harvest brings dove-hunting season, a great migration. For six days I watch monarch butterflies scatter across the Metroplex, dream their carcasses onto the highway, dream black beetles biting my fingers in your clasped hands. I feel a pilot light at the back of my throat, while the helicopter groans a few blocks deeper down Ross Avenue. And the magnolia tree falls silent, and the season concludes.

The Market migrates; the Market scatters across the Metroplex.
The Market dreams my carcass onto the highway, groans
a few blocks deeper into my neighborhood.

In the liquidity of late afternoon sun, a truck on the avenue clips branches from elms. What policy might we bring forth on our front-yard folding table? Deposit insurance? The return of Glass Steagall? Pull over. Price what you see. Privatize this rush-hour traffic. Look disappointed. The helicopter answers: pulse, pulse, pulse. These fences make a triangle, a shed of mostly shadow and quiet behind the boxwoods where someone left chemicals.

Texas Redbud

Up here you can catch small gasps of prairie between Bush Turnpike
and the North Central Expressway, slim grove of trees
along Rennel Creek, rust

and gray, gold real-estate signs, mixed-use zoning freaks forth
the Texas Instruments complex, still empty, humming.

Bells clang and gates lower at the light rail crossing.
The best word of the year: chokeberry.

If we had lived here as pioneers, waited for postmen, for seasons, watched crops rise and die, watched weather, the soil as it bleached. If we made a promise somewhere far east, forgave ourselves in photographs, read the King James, waded our silence, married our past, would we be better suited to survive this season?

"Forbearing one another in love," etc.

There are Cherokees in the bois d'arcs. There have been Cherokees in the bois d'arcs since we met.

Texas redbuds blossom into violet scabs, the last crop between the tollway and condos; the only text left before the ink goes.

Jerusalem

I took a nap during an afternoon thunderstorm, dreamed of snake

undressed and in bed, I read about a wrecked housing project in East L.A., bounded by concrete river; I read *Specimen Days*: wounded soldiers outside a hospital in Fredericksburg, sprigs of evergreens in the ward, happiness and raspberries. What a coin we could make from Whitman's soft eyes! So much moisture

in the air this afternoon before the storm. The bus stop smells of cedar, sweet huisache thickens by a ditch, pink clover edges my driveway—a kind of ransom note dictated and signed in someone else's name—

the sufferings most often deemed worthy
of representation are the product of wrath,
divine or human

Gen. Sherman painted landscapes. God sends swans into a storm.
Tarmac responds, asphalt responds, I
-beams rising into the night from the half-constructed Intel building respond.

And D. suggests I look at Melville's travel journals,
the entry in which he compares Jerusalem to a fly-infested skull.

11 Railway Lines Stretch from Chicago by 1861

an adolescent daughter slutting around
showing off   her terrible,   a pine tree
gone rusty   in winter time,   sun
seeps under her sweater,
ribbon development   and the public
realm opens up to cars
          deracinated country folk
could be wooed
by linotype, steam engines, turbines,
two tree trunks grope and bind
when you slice off a piece of crazy tail,   he warns me,
know what the fence post knows
you can drive
for an hour south of Charlottesville
watch a skinny girl walk a long road
recently paved, worried about loyalty
tar clings to fence weeds,
          unmoored from the nation
the thickly accented philosopher explained
we could find hope   rich light
on the stable roof
a boy from down the road
who will read you differently
who steps out of the trees responsible
for love, under a system that pays him
no mind   no heed   no blossoms
yet on the redbud
but space cleared for their coming

Woodsmoke, Starbucks, Gettysburg

You say smoke follows a fire's tender, and all morning the fire stalks me, throwing up facefuls of cloud and ash to make me feel far from myself in the mountains of Chiapas or a cabin in New Hampshire tucked into another's skin, where my legs might be longer, my sex might be broader, where I feel axe blade and muscled warm throughout winter.

But we are here, wrapped in our customary weather: cedar and live oak, flock of windchimes over Bee Creek, pipe organs in some vague cathedral of wood parasite and pebble. I build a fire in the rusted potbellied stove that you dragged from the hill to your deck. Great furnace of twig and newspaper. And even when we pass into full afternoon, I do not stop. You joke that you will slay a deer for me to roast.

Instead, we drive into town past construction cranes on the river, floodwalls of condominiums. The Sunglass Hut on the Drag has been boarded up. And outside what was once Peet's Coffee, someone has scrawled: More than this? Now there is a Diesel, now there is a Pita Pit. You tell me that the corporate plan for Starbucks was not efficiency but ubiquity, so that whenever we think coffee we think Starbucks.

Whenever I smell woodsmoke, I think of amputees under Civil War trees, Antioch, Gettysburg. You can travel to Georgia: fields of flags and Popeye's Chicken where Sherman burned plantations.

Our dog looks for bigger refineries, lays in full sun. A squirrel chatters in a sycamore tree. The broken boat on the hillside makes an impossible shipwreck, another's history.

O Sunglass Hut, we hardly knew you!

I-35

Behind the Robert E. Lee Elementary, I recycle my newspapers, magazines, ATM receipts. "Come volunteer in our butterfly garden." I am living in a new city. Nights I wait for Farid's call, his car, read from *The Teachings of Buddha* on the front stoop smelling of sewage and gardenia.

The old flower garden at Lee's Arlington Plantation included a summerhouse, box bordered paths, flowerbeds and climbing vines; all surrounded by a white picket fence.

Farid drives north on I-35. Henry James explains that after independence "America was required to construct, without delay, at least three great roads and canals, each several hundred miles long, across mountain ranges, through a country not yet inhabited, to points where no great markets existed…"

Summers when I was a kid, my family would drive from New Jersey to Disney World. Free Cokes at the Georgia welcome center, cigarettes from a roadside stand, a swim in some Howard Johnson's pool. One day closer to Tomorrowland.

Chop wood and carry water, the Buddha says.
Eat food, says the nutritionist.

I've heard a garbage island floats in the Pacific, mass of plastic, metal, wire, fabric, pulled together by fate and current—a phantom ship. Some say it is the size of Texas, churning off shore, a big paddle steamboat, wheel of dharma, satellite.

Tell me, my darling, you are at least on the road
tell me you are as far as Temple or Waco.

A Georgia moon can strip color from the sky, turn a whole landscape into its still-wet negative.

Show me the asterisk, clause at the end of my lease, something in between the butterfly garden and Arlington Cemetery, between cattle drives and I-35, wagon trails and Walt Disney, enough of the anecdote for everyone I love.

Texas State Fair

Ascending from the great midway: skyline,
radio tower, highway, rain running pink to the west.
Look south and there's not much to see, high-voltage
wires, trees.
        I've lived here almost a year, Farid says,
waiting for this vantage point.

Look at the pig,
from toe to asshole all the same pink-white.

Farid is asking about the lynchings again,
in souvenir photographs, a mark on every lamppost, every tree.

Am I racist if I compare you to the giraffe?

Birds shit on sawdust and hay.
The black stallkeeper
puffs his chest,
sticks out his chin,
at the ostrich,
broom and dustbin dangle from his hand.

Tell me, O Muses,
and observe proper order, etc.

Notes from the Last Great Civil War Story

Our dog licks my teacup;
late dog
days of summer, I study
new urbanism, racial
uprisings, cultural memory,
patterns of glassworks
on some foreign field of sand,
"high mortality events."
Death makes such a blunt box
such a 24-hour news channel,
video of a cypress tree
which refuses to grow
while a window
around the screen
goes from dark to light,
day to night.

Gen. Sherman's
funeral, Feb 21, 1891, St. Louis,
cold as the chill that filled
the general's lungs, former Confederate
Gen. Joseph Johnston,
vanquished at Appomattox,
removes his hat as the cortège
passes, saying Sherman
would have done no less.
Johnston dies of pneumonia
2 weeks later.

Woke this morning in Dallas
with Bentonville, NC
written on my palm.

Sunset on the First Day of Standard Time

So cool, you feel heat rise off parked cars.

The trees have their own calls.

Wrong flag on every corner.

Ask a question and the short answer is: "after 1969."

Nail Guns in the Morning

Nail guns in the morning from the street behind my house,
Outside: tin roof, cement tabletops, "vast maw of modernity" (Sontag),
the UPS man, someone has painted all of my windows shut.

The study of trauma comes shortly after the steam engine,
an affliction known as "railway spine," characterized by headaches, fatigue,
difficulty in breathing, reduction of sexual potency, stammering, cold sweats.

Report from Charles Dickens, June 1865, after train wreck:
    Wakes up in sudden alarm,
    Dreams much.

Storms this afternoon in Dallas
in the parking lot of the Target/Best Buy/Payless Shopping Center,
big chalices of rain, contusioned sky over the east, big yellow bus moving north
toward the dark end of—what?—

this weather, this fiscal year, this end of empire during which I am reading
the circulars stuck in my screen door, ice waiting
in the highest breath of atmosphere.
It will get to us.

I am patient on the living room couch,
let water drain from the kitchen sink.
Last night over dirty dishes, I told Farid
I would never write a poem that just said: *Stop the War.*

So frequently, I want a witness. Sit with me,
C. Dickens, let me tell you how bad

the food is on Amtrak, how a Pullman position
was a plum job for freedman, how stevedores once owned the city
hall, how Indians shot at us through the windows of the smoking car.

Stop the war, stop the war, stop the war, stop the war, stop the war.

Chalk Marks on the Front Walk

Calendula by the curb   an empty watering can

As I pull him across the lawn, the toddler
holds on to one side of his wagon
cups his balls with the other hand

Autumn wren on a telephone wire. A sliver
less of each day. What's next?

From a bird by the hydrant, 3 trills, the last 1 clipped.

Scrap Metal

First day of sun after many without, a robin pulses on a branch
    puffed up
    swollen
    one among many in this second-story thicket, window screens
taking on gold, an inheritance, left-over from another season, red in the branches
    of the not-quite dead.

I drive to the credit union, towards the late afternoon
skyline, dust and ozone, scrap-metal sky,
    towards the Taquería Chupacabras, Los Billares Sandía, Lavandería Azul,
day workers pace the parking lot of the vacant car dealership.

A slave, it was explained to me, was worth more to a master
in the years before the Civil War than a freedman in the Jim Crow years
—thus, the prevalence of lynching.

Texas cities get a little lonely at their edges:
    past Motel 19, Methodist hospital's blue neon crucifix, refineries, Christ
of the Nations Inter-faith Ministries. Dusk pales
at its hemline.

Copper light scores the westside of my chokeberry tree;
    rush-hour trafficopters
buzz over live oaks, ignorant to how much weight these branches might hold.

Yellow Finches Drop from a Plane Tree

Crosses of sunlight burn through the sugar maple
 each afternoon in little crucifixions.

Blue-black lake like an 8-mm film,
 its name means "high winds"
in a language not spoken by local Indians.

How does a tree move when it is angry?
I want to be angry like that.

In the Field

by the Osage-orange tree I saw the snakeskin, coiled, cresting
on clipped grass, black snake nowhere to be found.

With plywood, this husk of a barn becomes history,
stories to add to the building.	A family
traffics in burden and grief—what a mother carried for hers,
what a father hands you—

litigation in a parking lot:	weeds buckle concrete.

In Virginia, not family
	individual shaped the settlement
not bound by religion or kinship;	in Jamestown men outnumbered women
20-1, slaves by 1619, allowing a plantation:
carpenters, coopers, wheelwrights, millers, blacksmiths, midwives.

When Marion went with her friend, a meth-addict, to talk to his therapist
	about seeing ghosts, the therapist asked: "Do they talk?"
"No."
"You need to call me as soon as they start talking."

This room used to be a stable, without mini-blinds or surge protector,
	without barbed wire framing the meadow.

Daughter of Newark, NJ, I see loss
even in this view to a cow pasture—generations past larkspur.

Boys in Jamestown dreamed in petticoat, woke to armor.

In ref. to our previous conversations, to whose ancients should I direct my
	inquiries?

Specimen Box

on the wall by the fireplace
we can fill it   with stones, flowers, toenails, pebbles
of shit   or scat   or something else Anglo-Saxon   and indispensable.
No books on Texas   birds, no botany, the rock
is called a batholith, stands 1825 feet,
a large, solid granite dome   where white men
fled captivity, Comanche, Tonkawas, a sword-edged
tongue or a nettle you carry for miles.
        At night the rock moans its way from hot to cold.
Grasses by the highway grow bovine.
What is happening there? a harvest of lime?
In the luminous day by day,   the book was just interruption,
a record of presence, attention. Music
rises from the deep lobes of lung.
        Your turn to tend,
to imagine first a settlement
then something else, to wish to remark   ancestrally
to note in the deepbook a scent of sewage or sulfur,
while wading the tall grass to goats penned in our neighbors' backyard.
Logs from Kentucky, windows from a European farmhouse,
not the machinery I imagine
but the reasons why the water
tastes plastic. Self-reflective, palms open. I never want
to bother anyone with my presence,
        my, my, my, my, my
not even the goats. The fire pitches
its guttural song, wind makes a way through the porchwood,
movement in the musical sense, not transit.
        I rake the fire's hair, the grate

heats, a rib cage, pubic bone.
        A treaty of non-aggression between the Comanche and the first
German settlers here became the only such agreement
in Texas never broken, thus the guttural tongue, the fire
that moves to its end. I am tired
of tending and my thighs grow cold.
"I take SPACE to be the central fact to man born in America,
from Folsom cave to now...Large and without mercy" (Charles Olson).
        On the edge of the creek 2 or 3 yellow flowers out of season,
small earth-mover, tractor, when I asked her to name
the trees—she looked shocked—scrub oak not worth anything.
Does one need to tend to war?   Night catches
first in the thicket above the farmhouse, stones by the creek
moonglow against the field, help me name these constellations:
        cricket, lawn chair, ledger, rake. All day, I watch
the fire from the couch, but should have turned the armchair,
tended the window, dragged a kitchen chair to the porch,
watched the wall-mounted mountain
goat high above the kitchen cabinet,   Capricorn,
        eyes to the roof,
your eyes are so much better, so self-fixed, so specimen still.
You lack nothing. I sit close enough
to the window to stir the dogs next door.

A Photograph from Nature

George Barnard shot the capitol at Nashville, white tents pitched on lawns
       bombed-out trestle bridge, Whiteside, 1864

in the wake of Sherman's army Barnard saw trees split,
stripped as by lightning
thin bones   (metacarpals, dorsal, phalanx)
at the scene of Gen. McPherson's death:
skull of a horse   bullet holes
through chimneys

Ruins at Columbia (SC): pastures of brick: pastures of Baghdad, Belgrade

A woman exposed to pornography craves images of increased intensity:
       standard bondage to pregnant lady "jacking off" with mother's milk

Dallas skyline hemmed in neon   watch the towers become unbuilt

Draw my curtains early   sunset burns
in the belly of the bank building   tells me when to look away

Memoranda

Dear Mr. Surgeon General

Lately every time I drive over a suspension bridge I feel myself at a steely end, walking a knife blade, subject to winds, looking east as if calling out to the dead.

Purple clover along a highway is blood on my fingers.

And sometimes, Sir, I cry after sex, my mind like a plastic bag tumbling down Kent Street edging the East River, water tankers, maintenance plants; my mind roving the white line of a pockmarked road: soiled and mute, beyond touch or notice.

Once climate and geography were thought to cure illness. Rilke knew this and wrote: "...I left Paris, tired and quite sick, and traveled to this great northern plain, whose vastness and silence and sky ought to make me well again."

But where, Sir, might I go to await my convalescence?

When the Williamsburg Bridge rises up into view, sometimes a sigh will blow through a teamster. Sometimes you'll see a fly in an elevator like a feeling that has no place. You might wonder if it is some cycle of weather.

"Sex is difficult," Rilke explains.

One winter I lived in Williamsburg, Brooklyn. From my kitchen table, I could see the spire of the Chrysler Building peeking over the roof of an evangelical church. My roommate practiced martial arts. In order to test her threshold for pain, she never tapped off an opponent when trapped in a difficult move. At the foot of the bridge, National Guardsmen shivered in tents, while her arms purpled with bruises.

Some nights we drank licorice tea and talked about our mothers. Some nights snow blew in over the East River, leaving the Chrysler Building's spire to flail like a compass needle. Most nights I fell asleep to the clattering chains of a padlock coiling and uncoiling from a gate.

Dear Madam Secretary of Homeland Security

All day the tatters of a hurricane blow overhead: black swaths of thunder and slicing rain, marble swirls of cloud. Grass brightens against the gray. Steers call back. A cardinal and his mate worry through the possum haw. On a fence post, she preens. She cocks her head and calls. He flits and glides, carrying sunflower seeds from the picnic table to her orange beak. And when the rains return, they thread their way further into the ailanthus tree.

The Ladies Birthday Almanac warns: "Weaning children should be done when the moon is in Sagittarius or Capricorn…Do not cut a nerve when Mercury is afflicted."

Last night I dreamt of a porcelain dinner plate. I turned over small bones, picking at caramel-colored meat, my fork discovering the rust and gray tail feathers of that female cardinal I have been watching for days. I carried the plate into the kitchen to accuse. The black cook turned and threw her dishrag, shaking her head, shouting to someone else as she walked down the hall. My stomach grew sour and sore.

Madam, do you ever get the feeling there's something wrong with how things are run? Rwandans bury their children by the dozen. Tropical depressions spiral through the afternoon. And when a cardinal spits out his high, hard song, are we responsible to him as well?

What a time, then, to be an American in love! The Ladies Birthday Almanac warns: "Never plant under barren signs…Cut timber in the Old of Moon."

What a time then, Madam, to feel the cool remorse of dusk, when cornrows sway uneasily in the backyard, when a bull's cry resembles the sounds of a branch as it breaks.

Dear Mr. Chairman of Ethics, Leadership and Personnel Policy in the U.S. Army's Office of the Deputy Chief of Staff for Personnel

First, let me explain: My mother forbade me to walk fence rails with the Maleski boy. She barred me from taking off my shirt to dig flowerbeds with the Holloway girl. I kicked an overturned coffee can in the middle of the cul-de-sac. Storm after storm blew past the screen door. Standing under the plum tree's pale pink blossoms was putting on a veil.

In the hard soil of childhood, God was everywhere: in pitted sycamores, a vibrating clothes line, in fireflies hung still as lanterns from a Japanese maple.

One day I carved a whole landscape in the windowsill. Sun, willow, car, lady. Perhaps there were rabbits. My mother grabbed my wrist; rains broke; livewires writhed like eels through our streets.

How much loneliness must we inherit?

So, Sir, I grew earth-bound and cursed: a quarry, a construction site. God lagged behind in the pale light of swimming pools and pines. I took lovers and planes. In the desert east of Palm Springs, I drove past windmills flapping like angels trying to redirect traffic.

Yes, that was me kneeling down to take a birth control pill by baggage claim area three.

Of course, Sir, I can see it clearly now. Where once there was a thicket, I recognize three trees. A complicated song: a cardinal's call, a mother's voice, a wedding march. I want to undo it. Wind brings one bush to thrash and panic while another remains still as porcelain. Promiscuity, like a season, has its limits. Inevitably, rain weaves a sort of loose net on the window screen. Any woman of a certain age will recognize it as cheap lace.

II.

Isabella

The problem is that I always want two
things at once: to linger on Egyptian cotton sheets
and to be up at my desk hard drive whirring;
to sit on the dock dangling my feet in Eagle Lake
and simultaneously writing you this letter
about the ripples I send clear to the far bank,
how my toes hang above reeds and tadpoles,
about the family of geese that came on shore
yesterday afternoon and shit everywhere.

I am learning to row. Winds blow from the west.
An oar can act as brake or motor.
The ribs of the boat make a cradle.

Last night's sleep was shallow, and I dreamt
I flung myself over a group of children
with arms spread until my winter jacket
opened to wings. Men torched
parked cars. Police hurled grenades
across a street. And while we huddled
behind a Gap advertisement near a subway
entrance, my father ran towards
the barricades calling
another woman's name.

Morning, Dump Truck, Arabesque

Come autumn, we find a new way
to fuck. I learn to listen
using only my right ear.

On my bed, before a second story window: purgatory in brittle treetops.
Souls spread, water over branches, layer upon layer of the dead watch us.

Winter comes with morning traffic: a dump truck crests a hill
hauling plastic bags. Rosa Parks is wrapped in a white sheet, wrapped in plastic.

Who will sit with me
at the bus stop,
pray for the dead?

Come November I straddle your hip,
lay my chest across your thigh and calf.

I can see you over my shoulder, across a river. I see the back halls of your house.
You scream, a boy who wakes in the arms of someone who is not his mother.

As a child I watched beautiful women die on *Columbo*, on *The Rockford Files*.
I watched women fall from balconies, crumple down stairs.
I remember their twisted bodies,
pale faces, petals of hair.

As a child I learned to balance on one foot in arabesque, to contract my hips.
I learned when balancing to breathe higher in the chest.

The soul has no second job, no vacation home, sometimes it dwells
in the second story of our houses.

Come November
I see its dim flame,
when we fuck, headlights on a driveway
not too far from us.

Here in the Mountains

Wild thyme scents the grass. Birch leaves turn their backs against the rain. Now poppies bloom sticky with seed.

I have not seen a stoplight for days. And I am afraid I will disappear the way the earliest anthropologists felt after weeks in the field. Wood smoke tars the lungs. Language warps at a notebook's edge. I suffer from sun sickness: afflicted with yellow, insomniac. The moon slips into cedar like a communion wafer into a palm. Deer flies swarm my tent with the appetite of cannibals.

Black bears come down from the mountain to feed at the county dump amidst plastic toilet seats and crumpled windshields. Like me and the flies, they reject traditional notions of beauty.

We are trying to read a dirty world in structures of kinship, in gutted water heaters, in hills of plastic garbage bags like scenes from midtown Manhattan during the 1970s.

(I will call this boulder Bella Abzug.)
(I will call this birch tree Lou Reed.)

From the Ruined Concrete Foundry West of Airport Blvd between Manor and M.L.K.

Across from the airport park-n-ride, we walk on railroad tracks, hear a baseball bat crack just beyond the trees. Mixed-breed dogs rush to threaten us, teeth snapping at weedgrass. A shirtless teenage boy jumps down from the cracked foundation to call them back.

Robert Mueller Municipal Airport

And now you are flying, airborne in the thick
white sky, shedding gravity like an accent, like a way you used to sign
    your name.

I lean back in your chair, wear your hat, press your water glass to my
    lips.

Rain falls over the lake.

At the city's new airport, you empty your pockets:
a kind of downpour, a little divorce:
everyone can see what's inside,
an agent takes your file, your nail clippers,
a small pair of scissors.

The x-ray machine reduces your contents
to the barest geometries, cartoon lightning in a little box of storm.

Rain smells of rocks and concrete,
makes the air fat, makes the dock on the lake
disappear into a gray road, nearly metallic,
a color of something that could be "used as a weapon"
something federally disapproved.

Once I left a man, a marriage, a country; I picked up a new accent
wherever I went.

You say goodbye, empty your pockets,
everyone reads their contents, and everyone

can see into the buildings of the abandoned airport
through a fence around the parking lot:

the baggage claim is still as a stone heart.
And no one knows what we might build there,
no one reads what graffiti artists leave in silver spray paint.

Abandoned Commercial Use Property, 43rd and Ave. B

You write of our future in the birdcalls of pistols

It's true bullets whistle
a kind of beatific wind.

But the future is buried (Robert Smithson).

Look: a roof falls into the abandoned greenhouse,
        Brown's Flower Shop:
windows tagged, mold grows green on stucco,
tables in the nursery sit empty.

Seedlings make promises. Do not trust them.
In a semi-tropical climate, sometimes the sky grays in mid-thought;
Town Lake turns from glass to aluminum.

And down on its banks, flocks of monk parakeets explode
over high schools   and subdivisions.
Birds bred to swing in cages no fuller than a woman's purse
sit atop cottonwoods and utility poles.

Above them the sun makes a monstrous bulb.
We love each other
        and yet and yet and yet
Why should we want to confine ourselves in two's or five's or cities?

At Brown's Flower Shop
        wasps nest under eaves,
            unconcerned by the cracks around the air-conditioner
        how we enter, how I leave.

At the Lake

I stormed off and told him I wanted to change in the sun

squatted down, pissed on the rocks.

Sex can be such a lonely country:

"to be so full and incapable of emptying" he tells me,

branches cleared from the trail down to the water,

a small chainsaw lying in the dirt.

Red Constellations

On the lot where Brown's nursery used to be
construction workers lay a new foundation
in yarn and wood and mud.

The grackles must see it as skeleton, footprint, a half-finished parking garage.

We look for patterns   red constellations in the radio towers.
I see a Mobile gas station, billboard for breast-feeding, signs
that we love each other.

Farid asks: Will you be my family?

Downtown, a demolition site shines to a surgical theater, hums as if bone saw.

An image from nature would do us some good now:
bit of algae or a terribly smooth stone.

Dear foreclosed, dear locked and vacated, dear abandoned car dealership:

Freud says nothing is lost;   the mind is an ancient city
over which a 1,000 new cities have been laid.

Long letters are writ from shallow spaces   ref: skies above my kitchen table.

When I look up I see archer, I see dog.

3000 Block Kings Ln—Demolished Apartment Complex

central set of 8 steps to the courtyard,
small rock garden,
kidney-shaped pool, 8 feet deep,
blue flox, purple crepe myrtle,
white plastic laundry basket
in a parking lot beyond cyclone fence
Apartments for Rent
1–3 Months Free Avignon Realty,
railroad ties, cracked foundation,
It's all George's fault in black spray paint,
and black-eyed Susans
to which I feel no relation

Big Ideas

: this skyline these boats
on the corps of engineers' lake, glassy view
      and your eyes gray.

In this season nothing changes
not sky nor traffic,   the neighbor
      who lets his dogs shit in our yard.

You put the wet towels in the hamper, I told you
not to put wet towels in the hamper.

Dead summer just a pause   ripe/rot:
the light turns on the same
      but day goes out a little earlier.

      End of the workweek: a steak
pulled by a cartoon string

I'm talking about the weather, brother,
      and it ain't getting better.

A Blackbird Lands on a Wind-Whipped Branch

keeps flapping its wings as if still in flight. The lake comes in pencil. I hear sirens from the mountains long before I understand them, a fire in the forest. By the dock, 3 women tread water.

In pornography, the gaze drifts like a current, so that I am not just the woman on her hands and knees but the man behind her, cameraman fondling the Russian girl's breast, boy taking cock in his mouth.

This morning, the lawn mower bares its teeth. I hear a hammer from the boathouse.

Wind coils my voice over water, some trick of light or economics, tax shelters on Caribbean islands, a ring (like a promise) in a safe-deposit box.

When I write about my lover, I am writing about myself: the other part with hard cock, that loves me/loves me not. Early summer dresses spring in high-drag: windowpanes tremble, fuchsia peonies open many petals deep.

There are places so far in the forest you can always smell autumn, under canopy, thicket, even in summer. You can only wade so far into any season, skin—a gaze turns, voice twists

another lake, a winter twig.

From the Ruined Concrete Foundry West of Airport Blvd between Manor and M.L.K.

Days after we return with rusted metal plates,
sweetpea, a switch of cottonwood,
the tight-fisted buds open on your desk

—small blossoms of fleece that await our exposition.

Public Transportation

I walk toward the bus stop to the Number 1, avoid making eye-contact with a rumpled man who carries a plastic bag out of which hangs the leg from a child's pair of pants.

Somewhere in the city a man who says he loves me drives a borrowed pick-up hauling plumbing supplies. Some days he buys me groceries, some days he curses me, some days he lies.

Always be honest, especially with yourself, my father said. Always know exactly how much you are willing to give up. My father worked as a claims adjuster for an insurance company, estimating dollar amounts for loss of limb and motor ability, surveying the exact spot on the gymnasium floor where a boy became paraplegic. My father understood the fragile braid of a spinal cord. He said never negotiate from a position of weakness.

My father was born into a world that had no image for the cream-in-coffee swirl of weather systems, no notion of holes in an ozone veil, or the temperamental flare of suns.

Some people move like dull-edged storms without lightning without warning. Some people only speak after they have passed.

My father rode the trolley in Newark, New Jersey. My father took the PATH train. A ride on an empty bus can be a metaphor for a dream narration. I take what the window gives me. Here a gas pump, wash of paint over the crosswalk, a stop sign. A wash of clouds blows east until pecan leaves bend like wings over a branch of spine, half-held by sky. I want a different kind of weather or a new way to move through it as switch, as bundle.

Goodbye Twentieth Century

now the days tend
toward half-finished sentences
bring the mind to the porch
of the boarded-up house down the street
an air conditioner stutters, curls its lips
a bird on the lawn runs its scales
2 or 3 times
not a pill to get me through
it was the exhaustion, I'm telling you
sick of driving, she decided to make a dvd

Mid-State

There are no great cities left in America. Take Dallas, gateway to the West. Its skyline rises from the prairie trimmed in neon, insecure. In Austin, one evening, sitting in friends' reupholstered vintage living room, Farid confessed his passion for the "Real Housewives of the OC": their luxury sport-utility vehicles, their personal trainers, their cosmetic surgeries, their beautiful gun-toting children. Farid and I come from the working class. "What would be the male equivalent of breast implants?" our friend Phillip mused. The Dallas skyline edged in neon.

One August, I took a train to Buffalo from New York City: my marriage in shreds by June; my lover returned to his wife by late July. On the train to Buffalo, I carried a bottle of Herradura, a gift from the lover recently returned from Mexico. For 10 hours, the train shuddered and lurched: palisades, can't-sit-through emptiness of mid-state, dining-car Styrofoam. I arrived in Buffalo at sunset. Big cathedral of rust at city's edge: old railway station, sky the color of aged tequila, a pony glass of late-summer light. But it wasn't a train station at all. It was a stockyard, a Wal-Mart distribution center, a floating casino. It was a skate park for a while in the 1980s. It was an opera house dedicated on the 15th day of November, in this the year of the Dixie cup, in the year of the orange construction cone.

The bodies of my days
open up
in the garden
of
my memory,
America

Do you think Berrigan was talking sex or monuments?

Austin is a mid-sized American city smug with bumper stickers: "Dog is my co-pilot" and "Visualize Whirled Peas." After a long drive through central Texas, I stopped to piss in an Austin coffee shop/bakery. Graffiti in the pink stall read: *Men fall in love with the women they are attracted to. Women become attracted to the men they love.* And under that, scrawled in black sharpie: *White People Suck.* Austin has a large number of white people.

You might think the ruined cathedral a symbol for marriage. You might think the ruined train station some Tintern Abbey. Cars stalled in the freight yard. You might think that both Ted Berrigan and I should know better. Recently, I have lost a gold bracelet, a stone from a Mexican ring, my ATM card. My bumper has been tied to my car with string. In bathrooms on interstates from New Jersey to San Antonio, I have read graffiti: *Big Hairy Pussies Rule, Vote John Kerry, Bitch! Wipe the Seat.*

Manhattan has become the casino version of itself. Chicago is cold brick. San Francisco is water spilling from a glass.

Once I tried to avoid Dallas, turned east at Corsicana, found myself in rows of cotton surprised in the flat morning light to find that we still grew anything in fields so vast and monotonous.

Once Farid and I drove west from Dallas to see the coast of the prairie. Cars paused at a 4-stop intersection; the unimaginably wide lanes of a new subdivision stretched toward the government lake. 3 water towers, wide bridge and the gray-blue line of horizon, commerce in the black-eyed Susans.

A stalled car shone from road's dark edge; a river ran dry three-quarters through the fields, marked by cottonwoods, little gash, little Suez. Farid stopped at a gas station off the highway. Standing at the urinal, he thought he saw the work of rot or age. But what looked like mildew in the grout between tiles was actually the penmanship from men who'd been there, listing birthplace, hometown, way station, destiny: *Tulsa, Odessa, Abbott, Waxahachie.*

Memoranda

Dear Mr. Secretary of Housing and Urban Development

Lifting Farid's face from my hair to watch him come this morning was the best of the day. Light washed from his mouth. I pressed my hands into his temples. His scream softened his eyes.

All over Austin, Sir, workers dig up parks and residential streets to widen watershed pipes. Out of a hole at the edge of Shoal creek, a yellow crane slowly lifts a cage full of men, mostly Mexicans, who stand shoulder to shoulder as they rise into the dust-heavy air. The cage trembles before it descends. Under the men's grip, yellow paint has worn away from wire mesh.

Today, Sir, we have sun, and even the plastic sheets construction workers stretch to cover the dirt lot next door take on a reptilian sheen. Bamboo leaves flicker in the afternoon light. For nearly 2 weeks, the sky has been a damp rag. Life whittled to a slender focus: a sideways kiss, a single receipt, lizard disappearing around a concrete corner.

Now there is so much blue an occasional cloud screams out like a little Chechnya in the north sky.

Not even the grind of an airplane will undermine it.

I want a backhoe, Sir, that beeps whenever I move in reverse. I want a slow methodical warning, two chirps like a blackbird's caw. I want heavy, yellow machinery moving in my name and public works.

I want a backhoe, so that I can move my lover gently, hydraulically, a backhoe so that I can converse

with a powersaw that hums through the house next door.

Dear Mr. Director of the Census Bureau

Yesterday, hundreds of broadwing hawks moved in kettles over eastern Travis County, dropping shadows on scaly pines and glassphalt drives, powerlines and watering holes, sailing in currents of rise and fall, heavenly, purgatorial.

This morning at the Spider House cafe, a manager strings white lights through rungs of jasmine. At a table near mine, a girl sits with her mother and boyfriend. The girl pulls handfuls of bread from a plastic bag. "Tell us the story about the night she was born," the boy asks.

A cement mixer grinds across the street. On the sidewalk, a woman struggles with a sac of laundry.

"I was playing Risk," the girl's mother explains, "and they were letting me win."

Dante described the universe as a series of spheres and heavens: sphere of air and fire, heaven of moon and venus, heaven of fixed stars, angelic circles, rose of the blessed.

My mother hung curtains on the morning of my birth. My father untangled strands of tinsel. Capricorn ascended. I could chart all of the satellites dangling like a mobile above my hospital nursery.

Hawks alight on a high-voltage tower by the highway. Each scrub oak below them opens like a flower. Each city block unfolds like a square on a game board. This morning I can see the staggering boundaries of power grids and aquifers. But, Sir, they tell me nothing.

Sphere of the chain-link fence around a daycare center. Heaven of police cars pulling up to the curb. Heaven of winter treetops, barren and brittle; rose of the boy in a paper hat running toward the crosswalk.

Dear Mr. President

High above 38th Street, city workers on cherry-picker trucks unwind cables thick as a man's arm. They uproot telephone poles. Steel columns, twice as tall as treetops, bank over our heads like a storm front. Grackles percolate through live oaks.

What gears maneuver above us shielded by billboards and cloud?

In vacated spaces, the mind counts ceiling tiles, makes its own partitions. My brother takes measurements of unoccupied buildings. Once, he found dozens of dead pigeons fallen on the gray carpeting of a third-floor. They had slipped in through a hole in the roof. For days, they must have flown panicked through corridors and stairwells, under slack wires and cold fluorescent lighting. Regardless of where they lay, maggots eventually spindled inside them.

Mr. President, I want you to understand this is not a parable. In interminable expanses, God is a barbed-wire fence. Here in Texas, storms blow in from the west, plump with lightning and loosed leaves, tugging at raincoats, ripping dust from roads. Kudzu vines darken on the hillside; blue jays tear an afternoon to rags.

But, Sir, no matter what promise of voltage hangs overhead, a storm is a hand brushed over velvet: fields of emerald grass return to gold, a kind of wealth too large for a pocket or windshield.

Tonight, all of the utility lines above 38th Street glisten like bronze threads hemming in strip malls and practice fields, vapor trails soaring over intersections. And pigeons swerve from north to east stained by a light that resembles an emergency exit's red glow.

III.

And Suddenly It's the First of the Month

you mail the rent check,
watch jasmine blossoms fall from the bush
magnolias open like saucers from fine porcelain place settings.

How much longer will we decide to love one another?

An ex once told me if I ever left him for another man
he would wish us the best, then take everything
in our motherfucking house
                          —and torch it.

Take this view of the rose of Sharon at the far end of the porch
Take this crumpled paper napkin, this cork.

How much can any of us carry?

Just yesterday, a great blue heron alighted on the cottonwood
       at the end of Jim's yard,
right near Boggy Creek, right in the middle of our barbecue,
big wings hovering on the smallest of branches.

And all of us, even the children, turned from the fire to watch it.

Better than Paris

Good morning, I love you late   for a meeting   I am still
in bed our faces turned to respective cardinal points
        south/north   if we are speaking only of heritage,   degrees of melatonin.

Architecture shapes the body

no matter the square footage, I feel   a thin frame
      around me, a 1920s duplex: a thin white border
as in old photographs around
      this middle-class winter.

I watch a shopping bag gallop down of Ross Ave like some bad-ass cat.

Last night, looking for a parking space near the Dallas Public Library
I got lost, turned right past orange construction barrels,
      corporate headquarters, county commissions, convention centers,
      turned circles

in a downtown built in the late 1970s on the scale of a capital city
in some developing country, launched   like a wind-tossed plastic bag
into a future   at the farthest end of an uninterrupted plaza.

Door after glass door.
      Not a cop, not a vagrant in sight.

At the ruins of Pompeii, Melville writes *like any other town.*   *All the same*
      whether one be dead or alive.   *Pompeii comfortable sermon.*

Last night, I dreamt I held a stone with an oyster shell
        surface, some artifact of the soul
        5 years
the stone-shell gave me
        existentially, perhaps geographically,
        perhaps I should stop worrying about my IRA.

        Melville liked Pompeii better than Paris.

The Germans have a word for this
        feeling of walking across an interminably long space, this feeling
that we will never arrive at our destination: *platzangst*.

I watch a gray dove walk across Ross Avenue
in full morning
        traffic.

        If it's gray I call it a pigeon, even here in Texas,
        walking across Ross Ave   as if it didn't have a wing
to its name.

Hover

Day after rain and bumble-bees hang
up the Chinese Elm; butterflies
on spearmint; yellow jackets hum, wild
strawberries, too.

Beautiful, beautiful morning wear
your little edge of guilt, a slippery
thing, metallic thread   in your shirt, cassette tape
in the tree, a bloody little gash: bullet shook
walls and plastic bags on an overpass

Compassion,
I say, but the birdhouse is empty.
Lake, I want to say, but the lake gets us nowhere.
The honeysuckle has been pruned to bush.
                       And mother
is a great thing, gentle slope you
       trim back, power
over, woman with snake underfoot.

Most of the time I'm looking
        down whence I came
instead of up at the cosmos, next-Tuesday
-land, Cassiopeia in chains.

This morning
I count 6 hawks in the sky, 4
    swirling on their own
      funnel of breeze.

At the end of a field, at the edge of a forest,
where someone saw tobacco, saw corn and a slope

to the pond,
                I found you,
an easy history, one breath
lifts bird to branch,
clump of sage-gray moss in the highest rung
of birch.
              Nest or chance?

September's Company

In bed, Farid reads   *A Tribute to Ted Berrigan*
       strokes his cock.   At his desk,
I drink juice,   watch for weather on the creek
surface   nothing but water
       striders.   What are you going to do for me?
At the bed's edge, Farid's on his knees
—Not *to* me, *for* me: a dance or something, skate across the room
cock in fist   build me a tower —

We make mistakes   large public-works projects
for 15 miles under Waxahachie:
       empty tunnels wind, the half-made Supercollider in silence, mountains
       of Austin chalk line the roadside.

Still it's nice to know something
       's beneath us: surface of water, spider web along the window sill, weeds
on the hill bobbing in sunlight,
thin-leaved autumn: we grow short-lined
       when fucking   Farid says: Your cunt/Your cunt/Your cunt
Fucking modernist: big storms blow
       south from the prairies, big hole in the ground, a new book of poetry,
roads in Waxahachie that lead   to chain-link fence.

Short Lines

A brick is the next in the story

tell me what you mean, padlocked doorway,

collapsed ceiling, heaving trees.

* * *

Sunlight through traincars stamps a barcode.
Bird-calls modem.

All the great metaphors have been taken.

Yellow-beige lawn under melting snow yields
        weeds the color of telephone poles,
and on the Garden State Parkway:
a cell phone tower built to look like a pine tree.

Big Theory

A red woodpecker scales the live oak, while I sleep,
the phone rings   makes its erasures:
        a demolition/construction
        a dream in which I'm revising a list with my father—gone
the way of whole neighborhoods in the Bronx.

Robert Moses shrugs his concrete shoulders
        Robert Moses, I say, *drop the knife.*

In the summer of 2001, I lived in the Bowery, took photographs
of police call boxes,

took the train through Newark, NJ: warehouse, community college, broadface
    of the projects irregardless of choices. I was a lonely child, loved looking
at things no one would notice: Rahway,   Linden,   Elizabeth: the many-eyed,
bricked-up, gold-domed, on the platform waiting.

So far as we feel sympathy, we are not accomplices.

Thick rain   and tree roots knuckle the sidewalk.
            In Newark, NJ, the sidewalks were slate gray, dark as thunderheads
big bang   big theory   of charge/discharge.

As a child, I thought I could save my mother's life by stepping in front of her.

December

The overpass rises in plain dusk, nearly a cliché,

but I can see it unpeopled

the fly-over lane standing years beyond use.

Pigeons ascend to high voltage cables.

Why paint the train cars at all?

This is December   feed what you can.

From the Homefront

In my neighborhood, students from the school of the blind negotiate curb and
sidewalk, the early bloom of tulip trees, fire hydrants, a man
with his leaf blower. Their guardians watch from the corner, sipping coffee
from Styrofoam cups, shouting directions.

"Does that feel like asphalt, Terry?"

The mind observes the mind: a video camera,
a court stenographer. The mind walks sun-blind, washes dishes,
      writes a check to the phone company, gets oil changed in my car;
the mind makes a poem, right now it is making a poem. The poem reads:

SWAT teams exploded
a suspicious package
in front of the capitol
for fear   it contained
a bomb.

Other Denver Economies

Green tree in the yard and a dog
so skinny he fits through
the fence rails, tulips and the fence
that splits the tree.
Little white birds of this season
of circulars, children
walk home from school where they sit
in another language. And the hands they hold
smell of bleach. Spring is a chorus
in the helicopter's throat, the back
yard's muddy lyric; April is long division.
You'll find neighborhoods so poor
economists can't figure out an equation
for how a mother feeds her children.
Wage puzzle, they call it. Hello, season
of WIC, SSIs, AFDCs.   So sweet
these chairs on porches. Drink a whole glass
of tap water, consider the spool
of cassette tape dangling from a branch.
Watch the small yellow school bus, inside a child
rides strapped in a wheel chair, everyone
else in their pick-up trucks and SUVs.
Keep them moving, please. Barefoot sister on the porch
holding a black leather belt
            —you can make up whatever story you want.
I've got my stockings in my purse, bird in the gutter, butterfly
on the stoop. No—that's a moth. Anyway, she looked fine
to me.   There are other economies
in Denver. At a sex club on S. Broadway,

women pay a $20 cover, but couples pay upwards of $50, and a single man
might pay $100 or more depending on the night. Most of the time
we think of the body as fixed
in value—I've been 5′4″ for years now. Most of the time
we don't think of the body
and the soul satellites. Across the street
a Labrador sits in an open doorway,
the oak tree still clutches its autumn leaves
while its crown blossoms green.
It's not like any of us.

Up the Road

—bakery, pizza place with large parking lot,
county middle school/high school complex,
raiment of the working class, driveway after driveway.
       If you come from the south
come slow, take the business road, don't miss
our exit, a pill or 2   take as much   money as you can
home   with 2 bedrooms, 1 for your daughters
give them anything   they can imagine.   In this place
        you start on petroleum and string, writing out
the morning,   a tiny history.   What institution
did your family lean against?   Big engine of unions,
my grandfather, an official for the democrats.
Brown newspaper photograph,
hair slicked back   and ice
lines the streets as I write these.
       The streets should be shorter
sentences between us. We could string
aren't   you curious you   beautiful
breath,   a sky,   hills not too far
from now,   the rain sounds like paper crumbling.
Bring your daughters   to this place
tell them there was something special,
tell them we were something special,
our struggle has too few chroniclers.

Peach Tree

My dog bounds through the kitchen, dining room   a blue rubber ball
in his mouth,   he buckles, dives
as if to protect his prey   from my advances.

Cars take the corner in their rust shawls.

The ball is a globe of the world; the dog is named Moon
—the Aztecs could make something more of this—I flail
about half-heartedly, while the dog jumps.   Today I am tired
of being American.   I am done   with advancing.
In the utilitarian insistence of the Midwest, beautiful maps   show heat
and intensity of storms   red and greengold blossoms cross prairies
on my television screen.

Along the interstates, wildflowers red and purpleblue
planted by the former first-lady—
        Was this to make-up for the Tet offensive?

My dog does not know fetch, does not share.
I get moody, new wood, Rachel tells me. In spring
new leaves push to the surface. So much harder this green
then the soughing   off of fall.

Planes rearrange a low ceiling of cloud; all over my neighborhood,
single-family bungalows fall to townhomes.

Great cycles of weather and community, storms of capital flight, slum clearance,
bring Mexican construction workers to Dallas, New Orleans,
        to raze and raze

remapping in subtle ways, a culture, *querida*, corridos
from the skeletons of condominiums—
        a kind of serpent on the back of the altarpiece.

My dog rolls his ball under his paw,   bites at its side.

The peach tree on my neighbor's lawn is in fruit,
from blocks around people come, pick what they wish.

Laura Bush, what will you plant for us?

If I could stand on the roof of my duplex, I could map a circuit
of the peach tree's commerce,

        draw lines from my neighbor's birthplace in Zacatecas to those of friends
pulling fruit from her tree (Sinaloa, San Salvador, Lima).

        Those lines might make their own flower.

In the evening, storms blossom through the neighborhood
bruising fruit, leaving hail and the sockets where hail fell.

Car alarms cry down the street.

My dog whines out the window to his empty backyard

I could say he is answering car alarm, peach pollen, wildflower seed, demolition
dust, love songs from Zacatecas carried on a violent breeze

—but he probably just needs to pee.

I tell the wind, *Hurry*.

Windows, Roof, Wood

Newark, NJ

Ailanthus grows on the rim of a parking lot above the train tracks in a pile
of trash between concrete and chain-link fence.

From this train, you regard places you'll never reach,
storage containers, Quonset huts, bricks in fields,
warehouses the size of a cathedral,

web of wires, porcelain floaters.

"Detox the ghetto," a billboard reads.

We do not need to care for one other.

The years chainsaw, they gasoline first
windows   roof   wood
the face—even the beloved face—when wood pulls from wood,
a space between root and rotten leaf, tracks and trees,
so close so often I cannot see you.

Through a backyard: surveyors' equipment, cars stopped at a traffic light.

And the mind does not pause   takes the most familiar exit.

Ghetto with an international airport, ghetto with a Roman Catholic basilica,
          6 tracks across.

The years offer rot, openings, redevelopment,
scaffolding,

a billboard above the abandoned factory,
sunlight where never before.

A Letter to Eileen Myles

Tonight I want to write Eileen Myles. Eileen, I want to say, do you think I should have a baby? I am forty. I ask everybody I know and even some (like you) whom I don't. I ask the Pulitzer Prize–winning poet Robert Hass in the parking lot of an Italian-American deli in East Dallas. And when I pose the question I feel I am on a great ship slicing through the Atlantic. The sun cuts a rut across the ocean, a divot. Nothing seems impossible, just far away. Robert Hass says: Oh, you are trying to decide. That's difficult. We drive Robert Hass north of Dallas to Archer City. High school kids take prom pictures in front of the courthouse. Maybe it's the county seat. Robert Hass spots a scissortail flycatcher on a telephone wire. We drink sodas at the Sonic because the Dairy Queen has gone out of business. O Walter Benjamin! O Larry McMurtry! And all of your beautiful cowboys who did not have to worry about babies!

I've been sad, I want to tell Eileen. I've been spinning around with a decision decided. A body may be finished, but the mind strains. Farid and I have $15,000 in savings, $40,000 in debt. In 40 years, we've seen privatizations, a loss of price cautions, a rise in sunblock. Trees know how to make more of this flat gray light across the prairie.

I grew up in suburban New Jersey. My father took the train to work in "the city." My mom had a part-time job. We spun our skateboards around the cul-de-sac, gathered at the park at dusk. We smoked cigarettes and pot. When I went to sleep, a window-box air-conditioner clicked and hummed.

Now the city won't have me. I have gone to market; I have gone on the market. I want to come to you, Eileen.

Others have offered suggestions. One poet has a chicken coop; another grows kombucha colonies in her kitchen cabinets, she wants to raise goats. Another wants to go to Maine to study the contemporary back-to-the-land movement. What do you make of our economic avant-garde? We work in state institutions; we work for private collages; we work in offices with views to air-conditioning equipment on roofs.

Farid and I do not have time, do not have wealthy parents, no Girl Scouting skills, no collection of Foxfire books. One year we lived in a cabin on an Austin creek. A snake coiled under the sink. Day after day we hauled bags of garbage and laundry up a hillside. We were going to learn plumbing and carpentry. Instead we took our plastic rafts to the dirty water, watched the sun drop through sycamore trees. The creek became a mechanism of documentation and invisibility. No one ever knew what nested on its banks. When the winter came, we shivered near a space heater. When squirrels crawled into the roof, we left for a duplex in Dallas, where Bonnie met Clyde, where George married Mary Oppen.

Once I asked the MacArthur award–winning poet CD Wright about children. CD Wright said: Don't worry. These days you can buy a baby on eBay. But if we eBayed the baby, Eileen, we would still have to pay $7,500 a year for day care. We'd still have to find money for a down payment, replace our 10-year-old cars, plan our retirement. We are young and in love, all the movies say, we have everything. Farid says money rises as if a tall field of wheat; step in and it closes around you. Just beyond the window of our car traveling south down the North Dallas Tollway. No, that's corn. No, that's weeds.

Alexander Litvinenko

I found a billiard ball in the dirt next to the driveway
a tear-off, a throw-away, a non sequitur awaiting me this good-natured morning
beside the neighbor's rusted fence post.
Inside her yard I found room for all of us.
Move the planter to the porch, watch the snow melt from the eaves,
can someone reach the wind chimes, clear their throat as if beginning
        a ceremony?
        We swallow
unstable atoms in every cup of tea, fields of ice melt at the polar caps.
Find a blanket to lay upon them, a lead-thick thing like those thrown over a lap
by an x-ray technician before he slips from the room, flips a switch,
a circuit completed/broken   bones   as white as a silence
as when   returning from work,
        we reach the top of the stairs, call out: "Is anyone home?" Every day

another source of heat expires, bones from another
century. Winter
bends toward porch flowers, stills the wind chimes, kills the vine growing
through the chain-link.

If you swallow the right pill
your blood will glow inside of you, if you touch the right dye
it is possible to perceive any corporeal surface, a customs agent
flashing his light beneath our car, checking the contents.
        Where do you want to see?
Imagine watching your own blood switch back its course
round a bend, remake its banks, there
by the river in the darkest soil we might build a city, erect a barbed-wire fence,
        use any means to defend it.

Notes

The italicized section in "Jerusalem" comes from Susan Sontag's *Regarding the Pain of Others*.

References to Charles Dickens' railroad accident in the poem "Nail Guns in the Morning" come from *The Railway Journey: the Industrialization of Time and Space in the 19th Century* by Wolfgang Schivelbusch.

"Goodbye Twentieth Century" borrows its title from the Sonic Youth album as well as a biography of the band by David Browne. The poem is for Kate Greenstreet.

"Alexander Litvinenko" owes its title to the former Russian security agent turned dissident. As an exile living in London, Litvinenko authored several books critical of Vladmir Putin. He was murdered in 2006 by radioactive poisoning.

Other works that informed this collection include: *Photographic Views of Sherman's Campaign* (George Barnard), *Specimen Days* (Walt Whitman), *Travel Journals* (Herman Melville), *Geography of Nowhere* (James Howard Kunstler), *A Bibliography of America for Ed Dorn* (Charles Olson), *The New American Ghetto* (Camilo José Vergara), *The Collected Writings* (Robert Smithson), an interview with Slavoj Žižek in support of Alfonso Cuáron's film *Children of Men*, *All That's Solid Melts Into Air* (Marshall Berman), and *The Shock Doctrine* (Naomi Klein).

Acknowledgments

Grateful acknowledgment is made to the editors of the following journals in which these poems, sometimes in an earlier version, first appeared:

Big Bridge, Counterpath (online), *CourtGreen, Damn the Caesars, effing, Fascicle, Front Porch, Hot Whiskey, Kadar Koli, Mandorla, O-Poss, Ploughshares, POOL, Redivider, Puerto del Sol, The Rio Grande Review, Sojourn, Sentence* and *Third Coast.*

"A Letter to Eileen Myles" was first published under a different title as part of the anthology *Starting Today: Poems for Obama's First 100 Days* (University of Iowa Press).

"Dear Mr. Chairman of Ethics, Leadership and Personnel Policy in the U.S. Army's Office of the Deputy Chief of Staff for Personnel" appeared in the anthology *An Introduction to the Prose Poem* (Firewheel Editions).

"Window Roof Wood" appeared in the anthology *What's Your Exit? A Literary Detour Through New Jersey* (Word Riot Press).

I would like to thank the Blue Mountain Center, The Ragdale Foundation, the Djerassi Resident Artists Program, the Virginia Center for the Creative Arts and the School of Arts and Humanities at the University of Texas at Dallas for the time and support that helped me complete this project.

Heartfelt gratitude to Campbell McGrath and Denise Duhamel for their constant assistance and counsel. A special thanks to Rosa Alcalá, Janet Holmes, Phil Pardi, and Roberto Tejada for helping me to see this project through.

About the Author

SUSAN BRIANTE was born in Newark, New Jersey, after the riots. She is the author of *Pioneers in the Study of Motion* (Ahsahta Press) as well as several chapbooks. Her essays on industrial ruins, abandoned buildings and cultural memory have appeared in *Creative Non-Fiction*, *The New Centennial Review* and *Rethinking History* among other publications. Briante is an assistant professor of creative writing and literature at the University of Texas at Dallas. She lives in East Dallas with the poet Farid Matuk and their daughter, Gianna.

Ahsahta Press

SAWTOOTH POETRY PRIZE SERIES

2002: Aaron McCollough, *Welkin* (Brenda Hillman, judge)
2003: Graham Foust, *Leave the Room to Itself* (Joe Wenderoth, judge)
2004: Noah Eli Gordon, *The Area of Sound Called the Subtone* (Claudia Rankine, judge)
2005: Karla Kelsey, *Knowledge, Forms, The Aviary* (Carolyn Forché, judge)
2006: Paige Ackerson-Kiely, *In No One's Land* (D. A. Powell, judge)
2007: Rusty Morrison, *the true keeps calm biding its story* (Peter Gizzi, judge)
2008: Barbara Maloutas, *the whole Marie* (C. D. Wright, judge)
2009: Julie Carr, *100 Notes on Violence* (Rae Armantrout, judge)
2010: James Meetze, *Dayglo* (Terrance Hayes, judge)

Ahsahta Press is committed to preserving ancient forests and natural resources. We elected to print this title on 30% post-consumer recycled paper, processed chlorine-free. As a result, we have saved:

1 Tree (40' tall and 6-8" diameter)
1 Million BTUs of Total Energy
124 Pounds of Greenhouse Gases
599 Gallons of Wastewater
36 Pounds of Solid Waste

Ahsahta Press made this paper choice because our printer, Thomson-Shore, Inc., is a member of Green Press Initiative, a nonprofit program dedicated to supporting authors, publishers, and suppliers in their efforts to reduce their use of fiber obtained from endangered forests.

For more information, visit www.greenpressinitiative.org

Environmental impact estimates were made using the Environmental Defense Paper Calculator. For more information visit: www.edf.org/papercalculator

Ahsahta Press

NEW SERIES

1. Lance Phillips, *Corpus Socius*
2. Heather Sellers, *Drinking Girls and Their Dresses*
3. Lisa Fishman, *Dear, Read*
4. Peggy Hamilton, *Forbidden City*
5. Dan Beachy-Quick, *Spell*
6. Liz Waldner, *Saving the Appearances*
7. Charles O. Hartman, *Island*
8. Lance Phillips, *Cur aliquid vidi*
9. Sandra Miller, *oriflamme.*
10. Brigitte Byrd, *Fence Above the Sea*
11. Ethan Paquin, *The Violence*
12. Ed Allen, *67 Mixed Messages*
13. Brian Henry, *Quarantine*
14. Kate Greenstreet, *case sensitive*
15. Aaron McCollough, *Little Ease*
16. Susan Tichy, *Bone Pagoda*
17. Susan Briante, *Pioneers in the Study of Motion*
18. Lisa Fishman, *The Happiness Experiment*
19. Heidi Lynn Staples, *Dog Girl*
20. David Mutschlecner, *Sign*
21. Kristi Maxwell, *Realm Sixty-four*
22. G. E. Patterson, *To and From*
23. Chris Vitiello, *Irresponsibility*
24. Stephanie Strickland, *Zone : Zero*
25. Charles O. Hartman, *New and Selected Poems*
26. Kathleen Jesme, *The Plum-Stone Game*
27. Ben Doller, *FAQ:*
28. Carrie Olivia Adams, *Intervening Absence*
29. Rachel Loden, *Dick of the Dead*
30. Brigitte Byrd, *Song of a Living Room*
31. Kate Greenstreet, *The Last 4 Things*
32. Brenda Iijima, *If Not Metamorphic*
33. Sandra Doller, *Chora.*
34. Susan Tichy, *Gallowglass*
35. Lance Phillips, *These Indicium Tales*
36. Karla Kelsey, *Iteration Nets*
37. Brian Teare, *Pleasure*
38. Kristen Kaschock, *A Beautiful Name for a Girl*
39. Susan Briante, *Utopia Minus*

This book is set in Apollo MT type
with Eurostile LTD Standard titles
by Ahsahta Press at Boise State University
Cover design by Quemadura.
Book design by Janet Holmes.

AHSAHTA PRESS

2011

JANET HOLMES, DIRECTOR
JODI CHILSON, MANAGING EDITOR

KAT COE	GENNA KOHLHARDT
CHRIS CRAWFORD	BREONNA KRAFFT
TIMOTHY DAVIS	MATT TRUSLOW
CHARLES GABEL	ZACH VESPER
KATE HOLLAND	EVAN WESTERFIELD